Not That Witch

ISBN: 978-1-78324-267-2

Published by Wordzworth
www.wordzworth.com

Not That Witch

Written by

AMY LEACH

Chapter One

Aubrey woke in the dead of night, dripping with sweat after another nightmare. This one was different though, it felt different. She shook it off, got up out of bed and walked to the bathroom to splash some cold water on her face. Then she took herself back to bed to try and dream of something nicer and get some sleep.

The next morning, she got washed and dressed, still feeling the nightmare niggling at her. But she didn't have time to think about that now; she had to get to school. She stuffed a golden tiger's eye crystal and a green aventurine crystal in her bra, picked up her books and bag, and headed out the door to her first day in the sixth form secondary school at Castlerock.

She soon met up with Justine who was walking along the corridor of the school, if you could call it that; the building looked more like a cathedral with its high ceilings and old stone walls. Justine was wearing her wavy blonde hair down with a black floaty vest top, black jeans, and a black shoulder bag. Justine was always happy to see Aubrey and vice versa. The girls had a huge smile when they saw each other and gave one another a welcoming hug.

Justine was excited that they were going to meet up later to practice some spells, as the new moon was approaching. Aubrey said to Justine, "If you come over to mine for 7pm, I've got some lavender in the garden I'll pick and we can use it in our spell bottles. I've got a great recipe for a protection spell bottle."

Justine agreed with a smile that lit up her face and said, "I'll bring my white sage smudge stick to cleanse the air of negative energy, and my different coloured candles to seal our spell bottles."

She knew that bully Augustus would be in school again this term. It was the beginning of September and, although the days were sunny and bright, the mornings were getting a chill in the air that made you feel like autumn was approaching.

The girls met up for lunch together in the canteen; the noise of the busy hall was filled with chatting and cutlery against the plastic food trays. Aubrey and Justine had just sat down for lunch and were chatting about their morning lessons when Augustus walked past them and pushed into Justine, spilling her water a little as she was taking a sip. She looked at him just as he mouthed "watch out" to her as he passed. She wasn't scared of him but wished he would stop hounding her. "Why does he do that?" she asked out loud to Aubrey.

Aubrey put her hand on Justine's shoulder and said, "He's trying to be big and clever but really, he's just making a fool of himself. Just ignore him and he'll go away."

"I sure hope so," said Justine as she moved her eyes to her spilt water.

Their next lesson after lunch was one they were both in. Justine said, "Let's walk a few laps of the yard before our lesson starts," so the girls got up and walked outside. It had turned out to be a warm September day.

During the lesson, everyone was sat copying notes from their workbooks when there was a knock on the classroom door and the headmistress entered with a new girl who had just started at the school. "Please welcome Thea. She has recently moved to the area," said Mrs Myerson. "There's a spare seat by the window," she continued. The seat was right by Justine and Aubrey, and they gave Thea a welcoming smile as she walked past.

After the lesson, they introduced themselves to Thea, who was glad to be feeling a little more settled into this new school. Aubrey asked, "Where did you move from?"

"The city," replied Thea. "It's a little different here in Castlebrook than what I'm used to!!"

"A bit rural, isn't it?" said Justine and the girls laughed.

"It's beautiful around here with the woods and streams so close," said Aubrey.

As the three girls walked towards their final lesson of the day, Justine said, "Thank goodness for that. The first day back at secondary school is always the longest, settling back into a new routine."

They went their separate ways, agreeing to meet up later. They invited Thea too, but she had a meeting at the bank so she declined. "Another time for sure," she said.

That evening at 7pm, Justine knocked on Aubrey's door. "Come on in," called Aubrey as she was setting some lavender down on the table along with some little bottles and ingredients for making the spell bottles. The room was lit by a small lamp and candles spread throughout; the soft lighting was so soothing. They sat down at the table and set out the ingredients: some black obsidian, amethyst, rosemary, frankincense, and black salt. They sprinkled a layer of each into the small bottles. Setting their intention with some words, the girls said together:

"Negative energy, go away!

For in salt's presence, you can't stay.

I banish you with this salt spell.

So, mote it be."

Once the spell bottles were full, they put a cork bung into the top of each bottle, setting alight a white candle on top, so the wax burnt down sealing the bottle and spell.

The weather had changed for the worse and the girls could hear the raindrops tapping on the window. Aubrey made some cinnamon spiced tea and they sat down and talked. The subject of how mean Augustus was last term came up. "I really hope he's matured a little and he doesn't pick on me," said Justine.

"If we need something stronger, we can always try the other protection spell so his negativity goes back to him," Aubrey said.

Justine wondered why anyone must be mean in the first place and why everyone can't just get along, be who they want to be, and be accepted.

Aubrey's house was modern looking inside with cream walls, but the décor screamed vintage style, including a gorgeous lace and ribbon lamp on the side table in the sitting area.

They spent the rest of the evening talking girly and witchy things, including putting the world to rights, as friends do.

Justine left to go home, so Aubrey cleared the glasses away and then made her way upstairs to get ready for bed.

She wondered if that dream would come again tonight.

Chapter Two

The next day, Aubrey met Justine at her house and they walked through the woods to get to school. The wind was whistling through the trees as they walked.

Aubrey was wearing a khaki green maxi dress that swirled in the wind as she walked; it complimented her hazel green eyes.

Justine was wrapped up for autumn with leggings, a long teal vest top that matched the blue in her eyes, a cardigan, and a scarf wrapped around her to keep the cold out. "Remind me to wear gloves tomorrow," she said, laughing.

The leaves were just turning a golden yellow-brown colour and a few were falling off the trees, dancing in the wind in front of them.

They continued their way through the heavy-set forest until they came across a clearing at the side of the path. Someone had made a camp there; there were tree stumps for seats, a firepit made from a circle of stones, and a den made from long branches against a tree in a tepee shape.

By its look of neglect, the camp had not been used in ages so the girls agreed to go there on their way back from school. Tonight was the new moon.

The school day went by with minor excitement; the work was good but it was still early days in the new term back.

Justine saw Thea in one of their lessons and invited her to the camp in the woods. Justine asked Thea to meet at dusk that evening and she delightfully accepted as she's always loved witchcraft, herbal remedies, manifesting with the moon, and doing spells.

Arriving at the camp that evening, the three girls were all dressed in black, witchy clothes that included flowing skirts, corset-style tops with billowing sleeves, and cloaks with hoods. They set their bags down and Aubrey used a broom to brush away negativity as Justine picked up a long stick and carved a large circle in the dirt around them.

"Here is the boundary of the circle.

Naught but love shall enter in.

Naught but love shall emerge from within.

Charge this by your power.

So, mote it be."

Thea set four candles inside the circle; one in the north, one in the east, and then the south and west positions. She used a compass on her mobile phone to accurately place the candles before she lit them.

Aubrey, Justine, and Thea all sat on tree stumps within the circle. Aubrey reached into her bag to get her book of shadows out; she was going to write her intentions and what she wanted for the month ahead.

Justine and Thea did the same. Once they wrote their intentions, Justine explained how hers would go on her altar at home, with a clear quartz crystal on top of it to work with her intentions. She said that she'd been staying out of the way of Augustus today as she didn't have the strength to deal with his aggravation.

Aubrey and Thea agreed, saying they could totally empathise with that, as the moon can affect your mood so much.

Aubrey got her tarot cards out and shuffled them. She asked Thea and Justine to choose a card. Aubrey spread them out into a fan shape and Justine chose one and turned it over. It was the 'Ships' card which meant a long journey would take place or maybe wealth due to an inheritance or thriving business.

"Ooo," Justine said. "We are going on holiday with my family at Christmas, maybe that's it?"

Aubrey shuffled again and Thea chose a card. She got the 'Moon' card which denoted that she could count on success, acknowledgement, and promotion. It also stood for intuition, physic powers, and the soul. "I'm pleased with that," said Thea. The girls loved a little card reading.

Just then, Thea noticed a robin. "Ahh look a robin has just flown near; I always see robins and believe they are my familiar, giving me comfort that a passed loved one is near," she told Aubrey and Justine.

Justine said, "My familiar is my cat; she is always by my side when I'm at home."

"How lovely," said Thea. "Aubrey, what's yours?"

"Mine are my guinea pigs, but the one doesn't like humans," Aubrey said laughing. "Other than that, I'm like Thea; just nature and wildlife. I look for beauty in everything, good or bad." That's what people seemed to like in Aubrey, she liked to make people happy and smiled at everyone.

Thea knew she could trust the girls, so she told them about a dream, well, more of a nightmare that she had last night.

Thea said she was walking down a lonely path in the woods in the middle of the night. The woods were so quiet, but she could hear the noise of running water;

maybe a waterfall or stream nearby, she wasn't sure. She kept walking but had an eerie feeling that something was approaching her, and fast.

Aubrey looked shocked as Thea described her dream. It's the same one she had last night!

Chapter Three

The premonitions are getting stronger," Aubrey said out loud with a quiver in her voice. "To reiterate, you were walking down a path in the middle of the woods as well. Mine was slightly different from that point, as I then came across a pine cone and some feathers pinned to a tree with the number 666 written in red paint, or blood, underneath.

"I'm going to look it up. Surely, it's not a calling from the Dark Lord? Or if it's an angel number, it means that you are distracted and need to refocus on your goals and the universe is telling you to wake up to your higher self," Aubrey continued.

The three girls then heard a rustling through the trees, getting closer to them; it sounded like something running. Aubrey stood up and they all turned to see what was approaching so quickly when a wild deer

12

ran out of the ferns and across the path nearby. It stopped suddenly when it saw them, then darted off into the ferns on the other side of the path. The three girls' hearts were pounding. Aubrey sat down with a sigh and they laughed in relief, as it had made them all scared for a second.

Justine grabbed a drink out of her bag, took a few sips of water and then put it back. The girls decided to call it a night, tidy up all their bits and make a slow walk back to their homes.

Thea couldn't sleep that night. She sat at her window looking out into the darkness of the street; it was so quiet and she was hoping that the peace and calm of the street would bring stillness to her mind. Then she saw something that caught her eye, shining just under the streetlight. It was bright and she was drawn to it so she walked downstairs, put a coat on over her nightie, unlocked the house door, and walked across the road to where the shiny object was. Thea picked it up; it was dewy from the cold, misty night air. She wiped it - it looked familiar - where had she seen that symbol before? She took the stone inside to examine it under a better light.

She just couldn't place where she had seen that symbol. Her eyes were finally feeling sleepy, so she put the stone on her bedside table, got into bed and fell asleep.

When she showed Aubrey and Justine the stone, Justine knew that it was a rune stone. The symbol on it looked like a backwards 1, which meant water, sea, lake, flow, and renewal. At that moment, the bell rang for school. It made them jump out of their skins and they laughed for being so silly. Thea put the stone back into a zipped pocket in her bag and arranged to meet the others for lunch in the usual place. They then went their separate ways to their lessons.

A couple of weeks had passed and the three girls were walking home from school and talking about how their new moon intentions were going, as in their book of shadows they had each set themselves small goals.

Aubrey wrote that she wanted to love herself more, so decided that every day she would say one positive thing she liked about herself. It had been going well and she was feeling much more confident.

Justine's was to take more time to enjoy the little things, like a cup of tea, reading her books, and getting organised.

Thea's was to use more herbs in her cooking; she loved cooking and cooked for her parents often. Justine said, "You are definitely a green witch Thea; you use your witchy magick in your kitchen and cooking all the time."

"Aww thanks," replied Thea. "I just add different spices and herbs from the garden to my meals; in fact, I'm growing some wormwood in my garden to ward off unwanted evil or negative influences and I'm going to hang some in my home for protection."

They all loved crystals and the meanings of them. Justine was very artistic and naturally creative, so she enjoyed creating little spell bottles and had lots of witchy trinkets around her bedroom and altar. All the girls had so many combined interests, but each one brought something to the group; they had a strong friendship.

Aubrey returned home and discovered she had a letter in the post from her friend; she was always excited to get letters from Mae. Mae was a little older and went to university. She didn't go to sixth form like her and Justine, and would often write "old-fashioned" letters and notes by putting pen to paper and not just sending texts on her mobile. Mae, with her blonde hair, brown eyes, and unique fashion always looked cool and trendy; not in a catwalk hottest style way, but in her own quirky style. For example, she would make long gloves out of an old pair of thick, black tights and add safety pins to her denim jacket to give it a rocky, edgy look. It just suited her and looked fab.

It's good to be different and true to yourself.

The letter from Mae said she would be back from uni for the weekend, and they should meet up as she knew a photographer who would do a witchy photoshoot in the woods. Aubrey picked up her mobile and messaged Mae back to say excellent, count her, Justine, and Thea in. It would be perfect with Halloween coming up and she ended the message to say that she couldn't wait to see her!

Chapter Four

The weekend came around quickly, and the girls were all at Aubrey's house getting glammed up for the photoshoot. They were all wearing similar garments; Aubrey wore a long, black dress that touched the floor and a witchy hat. Justine wore a black crop top and a long, floaty skirt with a slit up one side. Thea wore a long, floaty-sleeved dress over black leggings and boots. Mae wore a black, chequered skirt, a long-sleeved lacey top, black gloves, and even blacker eyeliner. They looked amazing together and all walked down the stairs and out to the photoshoot in the woods.

The moon was bright and it was a clear night. The girls found a great place for the photoshoot; ivy was growing up the bark of the trees and the branches were almost bare, with occasional leaves falling gently down all around them. The photographer, who was tall and slim, greeted the girls and said, "Let's get started shall we?" He directed them a little on how to stand and pose but it was quite a natural, relaxed photoshoot.

Click, click, click, "Another great photo," he'd say. There was a slight breeze, so the wind took the girls' hair a little; it was the perfect setting. They were there for an hour or so with the photographer when the weather suddenly changed. The wind picked up and the sky covered over with grey clouds, so they decided to call it a night.

The photographer was pleased with the shots and so were the girls. He loaded his equipment into his car and prepared to leave, and the girls started walking back to Aubrey's house.

As his taillights faded, the night closed in around them. Suddenly, there was a blinding flash and a deafening bang as a bolt of lightning hit a nearby tree. Seconds later, with an almighty crack, the tree split, and a huge tree bough crashed to the ground, leaving an arc of smoke hanging in the air before them. They all screamed, looked at each other, and ran back to Aubrey's house as fast as their legs could take them!!

They sat down on the floor, exhausted from running and filled with adrenaline! "Oh my gosh," said Aubrey. "Dddddid you see that tree come down?!"

"That was so close, it literally just missed us!" said Justine.

Thea agreed and said, "I feel the universe is trying to tell us something, like with the premonitions, which I'm still having; are you, Aubrey?"

Aubrey said, "Yeah, I am, and I know there is a message in there, but I can't work it out yet. I'm writing it all down in my journal, along with my dreams; and your dreams are so similar to mine."

Aubrey poured them all some warm camomile tea out of a delicate china teapot. "This will help to calm us down," she said, as they sat in the living room around the roaring open fire that Aubrey's mum had lit earlier. They felt calmer already and started talking about Augustus and why he was so mean.

Thea said, "He's the weak one Justine; bullies are always the weak ones. Trauma of some kind, or something bad must have happened in his life to make him so mean."

Mae agreed. "Yeah, I've heard that too," she said. "Let's make a rosemary protection oil spray."

"Yes," said Thea, very excited!

"We'll need a glass bottle, dried rosemary, olive oil, a funnel, and a small sieve," said Aubrey. They added the rosemary into the glass bottle, spread the olive oil all over the rosemary, and the three girls all chanted this saying as they poured:

"Rosemary protect, ward and defend. Rosemary protect, ward and defend. Rosemary protect, ward and defend."

They each took a turn in shaking the bottle to infuse the rosemary and oil. Aubrey said to Justine, "It'll take around four to six weeks for the rosemary to fully infuse and make the spell stronger, but you can still use it now; place a dot on your forehead and pressure points."

"I feel better already!" said Justine.

Augustus came home from being out all evening in the bad weather, and the first words from his mum were, "What time do you call this?"

His stepdad came in from the other room and slapped him around the head with his hand, saying, "Your mother has been worried about you. Do you not think of anyone but yourself? You disgrace me! Now get to your room before I give you another hiding!" As he lifted his hand into the air for another swipe, Augustus ran into his room and shut the door hoping his stepdad wouldn't follow him in. He hid under the covers, crying as he rocked himself to sleep.

Chapter Five

I t was the night of the full moon and Aubrey decided, whilst drinking a cup of tea before she went to school, to pull a daily card from her Oracle pack. She shuffled and pulled out a card that she was drawn to. Aubrey looked at it and said, "Wow, fair play - a new start is coming." She smiled as she knew its meaning; it was positive and suggested something new and exciting was developing. The message from the Universe was about starting all over in some way; it also meant to forget about the past. She logged it in her journal with the question she asked and how she felt.

She believed it was a good way of keeping track of what was going on in her life, and had the knowledge and acceptance that the Universe would put her on the right path.

Sometimes things seem unfair, but one door must close for another to open. Another way to look at it is that you must make a change for change to happen; if you stay the same, nothing will ever change.

As Thea and Aubrey met by the edge of the woods for their full moon ritual that evening, they were just waiting for Justine when she ran over. "So sorry I'm late," she said with an out of breath smile. Thea put her arm around Justine, and they all went into the woods to celebrate the harvest full moon.

The three girls were stood in a circle around the campfire, chanting. They had a list of all the things they were letting go of to burn; Justine went first, then Aubrey, then Thea. After each chant, they placed their piece of paper onto the fire to be released into the universe.

When that was done, Justine said, "Shall we do a weather spell?"

Aubrey and Thea looked at each other in an 'I don't think we should' way but then said, "Yeah sure, what harm can it do?" So, they all stood up around the fire again, held hands, and chanted:

"Time for autumn spell to end,

Warmer weather quickly send."

They repeated this three times, then ended it with: "*So, mote it be.*"

They went home that night and didn't think any more of it, until…

Aubrey was in her kitchen getting a glass of water from the kitchen tap when it suddenly burst and sprayed right up into her face, soaking her.

Justine was walking home through the woods when she tripped over a branch, falling face-first into a stream. Luckily it wasn't very deep, but she had a wet and cold walk back home.

Thea woke in the middle of the night to it raining inside from a leak in the roof, which was coming straight through into her bedroom and onto her bed.

Well, you can imagine what the girls were going to talk about the next day at school!

The next morning, the girls met to walk to school together and as soon as Thea saw the others, she ran over to them. "We should not have done that spell!" Thea said in a worried tone.

Justine said, "I think you're right."

Then they all said together in sync, **"you'll never guess what happened to me last night…"**

That evening, Thea couldn't sleep for feeling like more things were going to go wrong. Sure enough, for the next few days, things water-related happened to them one way or another. Either a car drove past them, splashing them all with a puddle; or it suddenly began raining as soon as they left their houses; or the taps were spraying them when they washed their hands.

The girls knew what they had to do. They met up at 8pm that night and went back to where they cast their spell with a gift for the earth, which was a clear quartz crystal. They buried the crystal into the dirt and chanted a reverse spell, also apologising for trying to change Mother Nature.

They each wrote their apology onto a piece of paper and burnt them all in the little iron cauldron Aubrey had brought with her. The apologies would go into the universe and hopefully correct their wrong. "Fingers crossed that has worked!" Justine said.

Aubrey and Thea enthusiastically agreed. Aubrey said, "Time will tell, but we've done the right thing."

Chapter Six

At lunchtime the next day at school, Aubrey rushed up to Thea and Justine and said, "Have you heard the news?"

"No," they replied together.

Aubrey said, "I've heard Augustus is missing!"

The girls were shocked; they didn't particularly like Augustus as he'd always been so mean, but they wouldn't wish any harm on him.

One of the first rules of witchcraft is never to do spells to harm, or it'll come back times three.

At the end of the school day, the three girls decided to go out looking for Augustus to see if they could find him. "Just an extra hour to look around for him," Thea said on their way home.

"He must be somewhere. The local police have said he hasn't taken his mobile or money with him so he can't be far, surely?" said Justine.

They checked the local coffee shops and the library. They walked past the post office and noticed his photo up in the window with the word 'Missing' underneath, along with the phone number of the local police station in case anyone found him.

They finished their search by walking through the woods, but there was no sign of Augustus whatsoever. The girls said their goodbyes for the day and went their separate ways home.

Everyone seemed to be talking about the 'missing local boy' and the rumours about what had happened to him. Aubrey's mum kept saying, "His mum must be worried sick!", "It's awful!" and, "I hope they find him safe." Other rumours were that maybe he ran away or had been taken.

It was a very sombre time in the local community. School was a strange place with Augustus gone, but lessons and life seemed to, and had to, just carry on. It had been four days since Augustus went missing.

Over the past few days, Aubrey kept getting headaches and visions of a dark place with the sound of running water. She was very empathetic; she could feel people's emotions before they even spoke about how they felt. She often confused her own feelings with those around her.

It was a dull, grey day. Aubrey, Justine, and Thea were sat around their usual table at lunchtime when they all decided to go looking for Augustus again after school.

Aubrey tucked her hair behind her ear as she told the girls about her premonition and headaches. She said she wasn't sure if it was to do with Augustus or something else, something bigger, that would happen in the not-too-distant future. Thea said that her premonitions hadn't been so strong recently, but that she was still having the same dream of walking alone down a path in the woods.

As the girls sat around talking, Justine made a joke about Aubrey's guilty pleasure of having warm milk before bed, so Aubrey said, "Hey, it helps me sleep!" With that, she broke off some bread from her breadstick and threw it at Justine in jest, but it hit a boy sat behind Justine! Immediately, he picked up his bread roll and flung the whole thing at Aubrey. Before Aubrey could apologise, someone two tables away threw their bread roll and it hit someone else; then it just escalated into a full-on bread throwing fight between everyone in the school canteen!

Food and drink criss-crossed the room, direct hits causing instant retaliation and near misses generally causing more retaliation by hitting a bystander. Laughter and excitement filled the canteen.

This mass food fight lasted at least ten minutes before the teachers could gain control. By that time, the room and everyone in it was covered in food and drink. People who tried to hide under the tables to avoid the food fight still got splatted with something!!

Everyone had to help clean the canteen and had to sit the rest of the day in their dirty food-stained clothes with some very angry teachers.

3 o'clock came and a huge groan echoed around the classroom when extra homework was handed out as punishment for the earlier fun.

As the girls left the classroom, Aubrey said with a smile, "It was worth it as it was so funny; everyone will be talking about this for ages!"

Even covered in dried food, the girls kept their promise to look for Augustus after school. They followed their steps from previous days, checking the library and coffee shops. When they explored the woods, they decided to split up to try and check more ground.

Justine was calling out Augustus' name and Thea was checking off the path with a long stick, swiping at the autumn-brown ferns.

A bit further into the woods, Aubrey was walking along, also hitting ferns with a stick calling Augustus' name. Suddenly, she had a shooting pain in her head which made her fall to her knees; she shouted out in agony. The other two girls heard Aubrey call out and ran back to find her. As they found her and helped her to her feet, they all heard a muffled shout... "What was that?" said Thea. They listened and they heard it again; was that "help" they heard?

They nervously walked to where the sound was coming from among the overgrowth, calling, "Hello... hello?"

The voice back was much weaker, "Help me!" pleaded the voice. They knew that voice; it was Augustus!

Chapter Seven

They called out Augustus' name, and then stopped and listened for a reply in order to locate where the noise could be coming from.

Not knowing what to expect or see, they slowly moved through the autumn ferns, far from the path. They stumbled across a huge hole in the ground. As they peered over the edge and saw Augustus, he was standing up, covered in dirt. He had a few cuts and grazes and had hurt his leg quite badly; he was clearly hungry and dehydrated. He looked up at the girls. It was the first time ever he was pleased to see them, and they were pleased to see him!

When they saw he wasn't badly hurt, Justine had to take the opportunity to stop the bullying. The three girls stood around the hole, strong and independent. They looked down at him and Justine said, "Right,

32

listen here Augustus. We will only get you out of this hole if you promise, PROMISE, to not be nasty to me or my friends again. Do you promise?"

With an exhausted voice, Augustus replied, "I promise; just please get me out of this hole!" He started to cry.

Thea rang the emergency services and the three girls sat with him until the rescue team got there. Augustus' mum and stepdad turned up just after the rescue team pulled him out of the hole and put a blanket over him. They both gave him the biggest hug. Augustus and his mum sobbed happy tears. He was saying to her how he couldn't get out and thought he was going to die. His mum said, "But you are out now, and you are safe." It brought a tear to Aubrey, Justine, and Thea's eyes too.

The rescue team thanked the girls for finding him and so did Augustus' mum. One gentleman from the rescue team said, with a comforting nod of his head, "He's so lucky to be found safe and well. He'll be taken to the hospital to get checked over and they'll check that leg of his, as he's limping quite badly. They'll get his fluid levels up and he'll be back to normal in no time." Not fully normal though, Justine thought to herself.

As you can imagine, when Augustus went back into school, it was a lovely, positive day. Everyone was happy to see him safe. There was excitement in the air; the school was decorated with Halloween decorations and a feel-good mood spread through everyone. The Halloween party was just around the corner.

Augustus was hobbling around on crutches to help him walk until his leg had fully healed from his fall. The girls looked at him and thought he looked different. He looked genuinely happy; he even had a sparkle in his eye.

Justine said at lunchtime how nice it was to be at school and not have to worry about being pushed over or have those nasty comments that would linger in her mind after he said them. She kind of looked at him differently now and realised that she quite fancied him.

Aubrey saw that look in her eye. "Oh no, not him. I know he's changed but I think it would be a bad idea," she said with empathy in her voice.

Justine just looked at Aubrey and the air turned cold. She snapped, "I will like who I WANT to like!" and stormed off. Aubrey and Thea just watched in surprise as it was so out of character for Justine.

Thea got up from the table and said, "I'll have a chat with her," then left Aubrey alone at the table with her own thoughts.

Thea and Justine weren't in their usual meeting place after school that day, so Aubrey walked home on her own. She sent Justine a text message saying she wasn't sure what she'd done, and could they meet or call each other and talk about it?

There was no reply. All evening, Aubrey was looking at her mobile phone. She was trying to keep herself busy, so she didn't keep looking at her mobile to see if Justine had messaged back.

Justine didn't sleep well that night. She was thinking she had reacted badly towards Aubrey, who she knows wouldn't upset her or do anything to make her hurt or angry on purpose. She felt bad for ignoring Aubrey's message earlier, so picked up her phone and replied to Aubrey saying, "Let's talk tomorrow morning before school." Aubrey and Justine both felt better and managed to sleep well for the rest of the night.

Aubrey overslept that morning but just managed to make it in time to their meeting point to walk to school together. Aubrey started by saying, "I'm so sorry for upsetting you at lunch. I would one hundred percent support you if you wanted to go out with Augustus. I wouldn't want our friendship to end, especially over a boy."

Justine smiled and said, "I agree. I'm sorry I snapped; schoolwork has just been getting on top of me. It's no excuse to shout at you like I did though, so I'm sorry for that."

Aubrey said, "Will you forgive me?"

Justine smiled and said, "Of course! Let's never fight again." And the two girls give each other a huge hug. Thea hugged the two girls in one big group cuddle; they all smiled and walked on to school.

It's good to have such a strong friendship that things can go back to normal after a disagreement.

Before they all got into school, Thea showed the girls her journal that she'd been keeping with the premonitions in. She said, "Look at this. Over the past few weeks, I have been writing everything down and this is what I've come up with. I keep getting water, just water, lots of water, everywhere."

Aubrey showed them her book of shadows where she'd been journaling her work, and she'd been getting devastation, trees down, and open spaces.

Justine said she had been feeling panicky recently, which might be another reason why she had snapped at Aubrey. "What could this mean?" said Justine.

Thea said, "I think there's going to be a flood, but I don't know when or where."

Chapter Eight

Justine was sitting at home on Saturday morning and thinking about doing a healing spell for her half-sister who had been poorly with a bad illness. She gathered all of the ingredients, which included: three white candles, three oils (one of mint, one of lavender, and one of myrrh), three pieces of clear quartz, and three pieces of paper. She anointed each candle with each oil, then she placed the candles in a triangle on her altar. She placed the three crystals inside the triangle by each candle, then wrote the name of the ill person onto the three pieces of paper and placed them down by the crystals and candles.

With her iron cauldron in the middle of the triangle, she lit the candles, picked up the pieces of paper and, as she burned each piece of paper one by one, she chanted:

37

"Magick mend, and paper burn.

Illness leave, and health return.

I grant this now. So, mote it be."

She let the candles burn, setting her spell and intention into the universe for the goddesses above to hear and heal.

She did some jobs around the house but was so excited about the Halloween party later that night, she couldn't concentrate.

As well as loving all things witchy and moon related, the girls loved dressing up; especially for Halloween!! Not only did they own a lot of witchy clothing, but they also had some great accessories, from skeleton earrings to wooden wands and witchy hats.

The three girls got dressed up at Justine's house, and they decided to all sleep over at her house that night too. Justine was amazing at makeup, so she helped to make Aubrey and Thea's faces look gruesome and scary.

Aubrey had a mother of the dead vibe going on, with a skeleton face and black dress with a big, collared cloak and veil.

Thea looked great in a bloodstained nurse's uniform and her makeup was made like a zombie nurse, with life-like bite marks on her neck. Justine went for the vampire witch look, which looked great. Especially the red lipstick with her pale complexion and two stick-on vampire teeth which pronounced her real teeth.

They looked beautifully scary and made their way to the party. The three girls were not big drinkers, but they planned to have a few alcoholic drinks at the party.

"I can't believe the party is going to be held in a castle," said Thea as they arrived at the bottom of the long driveway to the castle.

"It's magnificent!" Aubrey said in amazement.

They walked up the winding driveway that the hosts of the party had decorated perfectly. There were fairy lights all the way up the drive and they were playing spooky music on speakers in the grounds.

As they approached the huge wooden castle doors, they appeared to open by themselves. The girls stepped inside and staff dressed up spookily welcomed them with prosecco or orange juice. The girls delightfully took a prosecco each and continued to make their way inside the huge castle which was decorated in a royal theme, with deep reds and gold decor throughout.

They followed the sound of the music to find out which room the party was in. It was in the ballroom, and it was stunningly enchanting. The Halloween decorations were out of this world, and some looked so realistic. They headed straight for the dance floor, dancing and drinking their prosecco. There were loads of people from their school at the party who would pass and say hi.

Augustus was there, looking good, dressed up as a devil with a red top and trousers, horns, and a tail. He had even used his mum's nail varnish to paint his nails black.

He stopped by to say hi to Justine and the girls, and asked if he could buy them a drink. They said, "That would be lovely, thank you."

Justine said she would help him carry the drinks and followed him to the bar.

While they were waiting for their drinks order, Augustus said, "This is really hard for me to say but I wanted to say sorry for being so mean to you, especially this term. You didn't deserve it and I hope you can accept my apology."

Justine smiled a warm smile at him and said, "It's really no problem; I forgive you and I'm just glad you are safe after being missing and you seem to be turning your life around."

He said, "Yeah, I am. I still have nightmares and wake up suddenly, dripping in sweat thinking I'm back down that hole unable to get out, but the counselling is helping with that and I do feel better. It'll just take time."

Justine gave him a hug and he hugged her back. There was a bond forming, but Justine thought that just friendship would be best. She sensed that Augustus thought that too.

She thanked him for the drinks, and they carried them back to Aubrey and Thea, who were now sitting at a table resting after their dancing.

As the evening progressed, they sat talking, only to break the conversation to dance when a favourite song was played.

The DJ announced it was the last song. Traditionally, DJs always play a slow song to finish, so the three girls put their arms around each other in a group hug, swaying and singing along to the song.

Chapter Nine

It must have been gone midnight when the girls walked back to Justine's house together. It was a clear, calm night. Eerily calm, the girls thought. When they were back at Justine's, they got into their nightwear, which was a vest top and jogging bottoms.

They sat cross-legged on the floor in Justine's bedroom talking about the night and laughing back at the memories made. Justine said how she really liked the fact that her and Augustus were just friends, and they will always have a special bond.

Thea said, "Aww," and threw a pillow at Justine, who picked up her pillow and hit Thea with it in a joyful, fun way. Then Aubrey joined in with her pillow, and they had a huge pillow fight with duck-down feathers floating in the air, more and more being flung out with every hit. Aubrey would sneeze and throw another hit with her pillow; the room was filled with laughter and happy screams. They fell onto the bed with exhaustion, partly from the pillow fight but mainly from laughing so hard. They lay on Justine's double bed and fell asleep.

When the morning came and the girls finally awoke, still all in the same bed, Aubrey said, "Thea, we didn't need our sleeping bags after all!"

The three girls walked downstairs and sat around the kitchen table for breakfast. As they sat sipping their cups of tea, they decided on what the plan was for that evening of trick or treating. Justine said she must take her little sister. Justine's half-sister Dotty, who, although she had been poorly, was so strong-willed even at 5 years old.

Aubrey said, "We'll come too if you like and we can do some rituals afterwards, as the veil between this life and the afterlife is at its thinnest on Halloween night."

"We can thank our ancestors," said Thea.

"Sounds like a plan," said Justine.

The girls loved dressing up and loved Halloween, so this was a special night indeed.

Day turned to night, which was around 5 o'clock, being autumn time. The girls were dressed as witches tonight, similar to their normal clothes but just a bit more accentuated and costume-like with overstated, dark make-up, lacy gloves, and all three wearing long, black clothes. Even Dotty wore some dark purple lipstick and dark eyeliner with her Halloween witchy dress and skeleton head-shaped bucket for trick or treating.

They all left Justine's house at around 5.30pm, knocking on houses that had a pumpkin in their window or by their doors. Or houses like the girls' houses which had decorations throughout, including tombstones, skeleton bones, cobwebs, and spooky music in their gardens.

They had decorations in their windows of bats, witches on broomsticks, dark silhouettes of castles, and spooky lights coming from inside.

None of this fazed Dotty; she was so confident and sweet going up to each door, knocking and saying "trick or treat" to anyone who opened their door. She would put her bucket up to them for the sweets to go in.

Justine told Thea and Aubrey she had done a wellness spell for Dotty, who had been so poorly for the past few weeks. She'd had her blood test results back that morning reporting that she was back to normal now and whatever virus it was had left her body. Thea and Aubrey were so pleased as they knew it was a worrying time for Justine and her family.

After knocking on lots of doors in the neighbourhood and Dotty's trick or treat bucket getting heavy with the weight of sweets in it, Justine said she would take Dotty back home and come back out afterwards and meet the girls. So, the girls took a slow walk to their camp in the woods and about 15 minutes later, Justine showed up with her torch.

It was a dark night; they couldn't see the moon through the cloudy sky. "Looks like rain soon," said Aubrey. "Let's hope it holds off for a little bit."

With the fire lit in the middle of the camp, the girls brought an apple cut in half to reveal the five-point star in the middle of the apple. This would be used as an offering when the veil between this life and the next was at its thinnest.

The girls stood around the fire pit, chanting. Arms out, holding hands, eyes closed to help visualise their chant: "*beauty, healing, love, luck, peace, power, strength*" over and over, getting quicker and quicker so it was just a mumbled sound. A sudden gust of wind blew past the girls, and a voice said "run". They stopped their chant. Eyes wide open, they looked around almost surprised. "Did you hear that?" said Thea.

Justine said, "It sounded like a voice, but I didn't hear what they said."

Aubrey said, "It sounded like 'run' to me."

Thea agreed. They got a strong intuition to leave, so they put the fire out, gathered their things, and left straight away.

Chapter Ten

The girls hurried back to their own homes, briefly saying their goodbyes for the night, and confirming they'd text each other later. They went their separate ways, all walking fast to get to the safety of their rooms.

Aubrey got home and shut the door with her back against it, so she could calm her racing heartbeat. Oh my goodness, she thought; did they hear that right? But it didn't matter. They knew their intuition was always right and they followed that.

Thea got home, shut the door, and ran into the lounge to tell her parents about what had happened that night.

Justine didn't go home; she wanted to see if anything was going to happen, so she climbed up to the highest

47

hill overlooking the sleepy town. The rain was coming down now, thick and heavy drops hitting her face and body. She took shelter under some trees at the top of the hill, thinking perhaps this wasn't one of her smartest ideas. She should have gone home like Aubrey and Thea, but her curiosity had gotten the better of her.

Looking down at the valley, Justine could see movement. "What is that?" she said to herself. Seconds later, she realised it was a huge tidal wave heading down towards the houses and the school. "Oh my gosh!" She stood stunned, unable to move or shout.

Her mind was racing with questions: "What was happening?" "Where did that water come from?" "I need to warn my family and friends but there's no time!" She quickly grabbed her mobile and dialled home ...

The water ran through the town's roads, taking cars with it as it flooded through the streets. Lights started coming on in houses when they heard the water pouring into their homes, and there were sounds of metal on metal colliding from cars being swept away.

Thea and her family were downstairs when the flood hit their home. They tried to stop the water from coming in by putting draught excluders and other objects in front of the doors and windows.

Aubrey was upstairs in her parents' bedroom telling them about the voice and her intuition when she heard a commotion outside. She ran to the window to look out and saw cars and garden sheds sliding past her home. By this point, her parents were at the window looking out in shock.

Aubrey ran downstairs to collect her guinea pigs and brought them upstairs, where hopefully they would be safe. No one knew if the water would wash their houses away, or how deep the water would get.

Thea was just about to ring 999 for the emergency services, when the power went off and they were sat in darkness. She just heard an engaged tone on the other end of the phone. Thea started to cry and, using the torch on her mobile phone, crawled over to her family who were looking out of the window to see if the water was going to get any higher.

Justine ran down the hill towards the raging water and her home. She wondered how she was going to get across the water. Feeling all alone, she looked around for the shallowest place to cross and she stepped into the water. It was bitter cold and it was running fast around her knees and thighs. Before she knew it, the water was up to her shoulders.

Justine almost got to the other side, when debris floated past and pushed her off her feet. She was floating away with the current and swell of the water. She scrambled to the side to grab onto something, but she kept slipping into the water and floating down the wide streets...

Thea and Aubrey separately had a vision that Justine was in trouble, and they simultaneously rushed out to try and find her.

Thea's vision was of Justine being pulled by a hand; she wasn't sure if she was being pulled under the water or pulled to safety.

Aubrey's vision was that Justine must swim and aim for the right-hand side of where she was.

The girls got as far as their front gates, but it was too dangerous to go any further. In tune with each other, both Thea and Aubrey stood still and calm in the cold, racing water. They put their fingers together to make a triangle shape on their foreheads where their third eye was.

They telepathically sent each of their visions to Justine, not knowing at that time the other friend was doing the same.

Justine kept going under the water and scrambling up for air, her arms frantically swimming to keep her afloat. She had the intuition to aim for the right-hand side of the street. She swam frantically against the current and flow of the water, not knowing if it was the right thing to do. Justine was scared and just trying to survive.

Chapter Eleven

Just then, a hand reached down and grabbed her hand. With the other hand, she grabbed the wall of someone's garden and pulled herself up where the water couldn't quite reach. "Thank you so much," Justine said to the hero who had saved her.

He smiled and said, "You're welcome." It could have been the danger, the adrenaline, or the waning crescent moon in Virgo, but there was an instant spark between them as their eyes met. The stranger said, "Hi, my name is Brendan. Nice to meet you."

"Oh my goodness, I thought I was going to be swept away then!" Justine said, with tears in her eyes.

Brendan asked, "Where are you heading to? I don't know the area as I've just come to visit my grandma for the week."

Justine said, "I'm trying to get to my home in Victoria Street."

"We will go together," Brendan said. "My grandma is upstairs safe; I want to make sure you get to your family safe."

Justine said with an emotional smile, "Thank you so much; you don't know how appreciated that is."

The rain was getting a bit lighter now, but still stinging their faces as they carefully made their way to Justine's house. When they arrived there, Justine knocked on the downstairs window. The window opened upstairs and Justine's mum peered out. She was so happy to see her daughter safe and well, although soaked through.

"I'll come down to open the window and let you in," said Justine's mum, a small petite lady with blonde hair like her daughter's. Justine climbed through the open window and turned to thank Brendan again. Brendan said, "See you around," with a smile that lit up his green eyes. He was of slim build with light brown hair, although the rain made it look darker. Brendan turned away and disappeared into the night.

As Justine and her mum waded through the water-soaked lounge to the hallway that led upstairs, she asked if Dotty was OK. When her mum confirmed that Dotty was safely sleeping in their bed, Justine sobbed into her mum's arms with relief.

It was a long night for families in the town. Fire rescue was sent to help many in the community; the rest seemed to be all huddled in one room upstairs, either waiting to be saved or waiting for the water level to reduce. It was so dark with all the power off in town.

By morning, the water had started to recede, and just a trickle was running down the street. Aubrey saw on the news report on her mobile that the dam a few miles away had burst, causing all the water to flow straight down into Castlebrook. The heavy rainstorm that night hadn't helped either.

Thea and her family nervously walked downstairs to see what was left of the ground floor of their house. Thea messaged Aubrey saying, "Have you heard from Justine? She's not messaged since we left her at the parting of the woods."

Aubrey replied, "I'm sure she will message when she can; she could be saving battery or may have lost her phone in the water."

Both Aubrey and Thea's intuition didn't tell them that Justine was hurt or anything bad, so they weren't that worried, but would both feel better if they heard from her.

Later that day, when the water had subsided, Aubrey went out for a walk to see what devastation had happened in the small town and to walk to Justine's, if she was able to.

There was still no power to the town at all. The emergency services were using generators to pump all of the water out from inside people's homes and shops.

Aubrey said with a joke in her tone, "You watch, there will still be school tomorrow!" Her parents laughed. She knew there really wouldn't be any school, at least until the electricity was back on.

The clean-up of the houses only took a few days, as a lot of people had put furniture upstairs to avoid water damage. The streets, however, would take longer, but everyone worked together and brought a real community spirit to Castlebrook.

The girls hadn't seen each other since the flood, but with the power on again, they had spoken to Justine on the landline and were pleased that no one had been hurt.

It was the Thursday before Bonfire Night, and a new moon in Scorpio was approaching.

The girls had arranged to meet at their usual spot and walk to their camp. When they saw each other, they cried happy tears as they realised that it could have been a different situation if Justine hadn't been saved by the stranger.

As they walked through the woods, they could see disruption. Some trees had been overwhelmed by the flood, and it was still very wet underfoot.

They made it to their camp, which had escaped serious damage; nothing that couldn't be fixed anyway.

They set their new moon intentions and wishes, and how they would achieve these, by writing them down and burning them in the iron cauldron. Then they each had a visualisation ceremony.

Sometimes, they worked together to make it more powerful but other times, they just worked alone.

Justine felt a little down and out of sorts after the flood, so she wanted to make a happiness talisman.

She got the bits out of her bag and, sitting on the log, she got the amber she had charged in the sunshine earlier that day, and the jewellery wire. She wrapped the wire around the amber six times as it was a solar number. She chanted:

"Bring me happiness, in my time of need.

Banish my blues out to sea.

Bring me joy everlasting, and make my sorrows ever fleeting.

So, mote it be."

She put the talisman in her pocket to keep with her so she could continue to use it whenever she felt down.

The girls decided to pack up and call it an evening. It was Bonfire Night tomorrow and they would see each other then. They said their goodnights at the woods' edge and went their separate ways home.

Chapter Twelve

I t was Bonfire Night and all over Castlebrook, the town gathered for a fireworks display. It was going to be just what the town needed after the upset of the flood.

Aubrey called for Justine and then both girls went to call for Thea. They walked to the field where the bonfire and fireworks were being held; they were wrapped up warm as there was a chill in the air. The girls decided to get a hot chocolate to warm them up before watching the fireworks.

After stopping by the coffee shop, they walked across the field towards the raging bonfire, which had most of the town's water-damaged furniture on and was burning nicely.

The girls warmed their gloved fingers on their cups.

Aubrey said her premonitions had stopped. Thea said, "Yeah, my premonitions have stopped too."

Justine said, "I'm so glad that's over and we can get back to normal and rebuild the town to make it even better."

They got as close to the roaring fire as possible without burning, to warm up. The glow of the fire was reflecting on the girls' faces, flames flickering and popping in the cold night's air.

Justine got a tap on the shoulder; she turned around and it was Brendan standing there with a big smile. He said, "I was hoping to bump into you again."

Justine couldn't believe it. "I was hoping to see you again too," she said, surprised. "How's your grandma after the flood?"

"She's good. Turns out I'm staying with her for a bit longer," he said. "My family are moving up this way, so I'll be looking to open a shop here." Justine smiled and nodded in agreement.

Brendan continued, "Maybe you can show me around?"

"I would love that," Justine said with the biggest smile, locking his gaze as they stared at each other smiling. "What do you sell?" Justine asked.

Brendan said, "Well, I'm interested in witchcraft and magic; like crystals, gemstones, spell books, herbs and spices, candles, that sort of thing."

The girls couldn't believe it. "We'd love a shop like that locally. With the history here, it should be a huge success," Aubrey said.

The first bang of the fireworks interrupted their gaze. They turned to look. They were so pretty, like shooting stars going up into the sky with a bang, pop, or fizz.

The different coloured fireworks lit up everyone's faces, and just then, in that moment they knew everything would be OK.

After the fireworks had finished, Brendan asked Justine for her mobile number. She smiled and gave her number to Brendan, knowing he would call later. Aubrey and Thea smiled at Justine.

There was something magical about this time of the year; with the nights drawing in, the crisp air and the leaves falling from the trees, nature and earth were going to sleep for the winter. But magick never sleeps or stops, and the girls knew they had an unmistakable bond that nothing could break.

The three girls held hands and walked into the woods, knowing that where they were right now, in this very moment, was where they should be. They were on the right path. They disappeared into the woods to make some more magick.

The End

ACKNOWLEDGMENTS

I wrote this book for children growing up in today's world. To my son, daughter, niece and nephews, I want to say; these can be hard times but know you are strong. You have family and friends who love you and with that love, you will achieve great things. Among the hard times, there is so much joy, fun, and laughter ahead; and as my mum always said, you never know what's around the corner.

Live your best life that is true to you.

This book is based on some lifelong friends who share the same witchcraft interests. You are women who fix another woman's crown; and we might go weeks, even years, without seeing each other, but it's like we've never been apart and you always inspire me.

The support I've had from my family and friends for writing this book has been so generous, and I want to thank you all from the bottom of my heart.

I also would like to thank Jo at The Grammar Guru for her hard work editing my book and continued support, along with Doug and his team at Wordzworth who have provided excellent service and guidance.

Link to free bookmark on the next page:

https://www.amytheauthor.co.uk/